1984
THE YEAR
I WAS BORN

A Daily Record of Events
Canadian Edition

Compiled by LINDA GRANFIELD
Illustrated by BILL SLAVIN

BIRTH CERTIFICATE

Name: _____

Birthdate: _____

Time: _____

Place: _____

Weight: _____

Length: _____

Mother's name: _____

Father's name: _____

Kids Can Press Ltd.
Toronto

For Valerie Hussey and Ricky Englander who, in 1984, invited me to join the merry band of Canadian children's writers.

The author wishes to thank the Social Sciences staff of the central branch of the Mississauga (Ontario) Public Library for their aid and co-operation in the research of this book.

Printed by permission of Signpost Books, Ltd., England

First Canadian edition published 1996

Canadian Cataloguing in Publication Data

Granfield, Linda
     1984, the year I was born : a daily record of events

Canadian ed.
ISBN 1-55074-309-0

1. Nineteen eighty-four, A.D. - Chronology - Juvenile literature.
2. Canada - History - 1963-   - Chronology - Juvenile literature.
I. Slavin, Bill.   II. Title.

FC630.G73   1996 j971.064'7   C96-930729-2
F1034.2.G73   1996

Stamps reproduced courtesy of Canada Post Corporation.

Kids Can Press Ltd.
29 Birch Avenue
Toronto, Ontario, Canada
M4V 1E2

Edited by Trudee Romanek
Designed by Esperança Melo
Printed in Hong Kong

96 0 9 8 7 6 5 4 3 2 1

A Week of Birthdays

Monday's child is fair of face,
Tuesday's child is full of grace,
Wednesday's child is full of woe,
Thursday's child has far to go,
Friday's child is loving and giving,
Saturday's child works hard for its living,
But the child that's born on the Sabbath day
Is bonny and blithe, and good and gay.

The Days of the Week

Sunday — the
sun's day

Monday — the
moon's day

Tuesday — day of Tiu,
or Tyr, the Norse god of
war and the sky

Wednesday — Woden's
day (Woden, or Odin,
was the chief Norse god)

Thursday — Thor's day
(in Norse mythology, Thor
was the god of thunder)

Friday — Freya's day
(Freya was a wife of
Odin and the goddess
of love and beauty)

Saturday — Saturn's day
(in Roman mythology,
Saturn was a harvest god)

The Months

January — the month of Janus, Roman god of doorways, who had two faces looking in opposite directions

February — the month of februa, a Roman festival of purification

March — the month of Mars, the Roman god of war

April — the month of Venus, the Roman goddess of love

May — the month of Maia, the Roman goddess of spring

June — the month of Juno, the principal Roman goddess

July — the month of Roman emperor Julius Caesar

August — the month of Roman emperor Augustus

September — the seventh (*septem*) month of the old Roman calendar

October — the eighth (*octo*) month of the old Roman calendar

November — the ninth (*novem*) month of the old Roman calendar

December — the tenth (*decem*) month of the old Roman calendar

Birthstones and Flowers

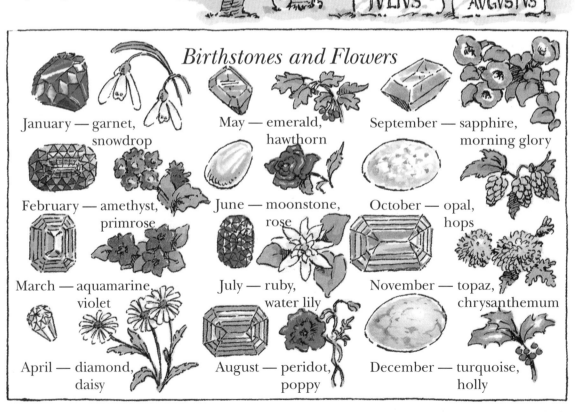

January — garnet, snowdrop

February — amethyst, primrose

March — aquamarine, violet

April — diamond, daisy

May — emerald, hawthorn

June — moonstone, rose

July — ruby, water lily

August — peridot, poppy

September — sapphire, morning glory

October — opal, hops

November — topaz, chrysanthemum

December — turquoise, holly

Extra! Extra!

Orwell's Famous 1984 Arrives

In 1948, English writer George Orwell randomly chose the time setting for his new science fiction novel by reversing the year's numbers, and titled the book *1984*. It is the bleak story of Winston Smith and the power-hungry world he sees around him. The book became so popular that it sold millions of copies in 61 languages, and expressions from the novel, such as "Big Brother is watching you," have become part of our language. Orwell was not *trying* to predict the future, but some of his ideas (data banks, satellite cameras) had become a reality by 1984.

Top Languages in Canada

There were lots of languages spoken in Canada in 1984, but those heard most often were English (about 15 million people), French (more than 6 million), Italian (530 000), German (523 000), and Ukrainian (292 000).

Trivia tidbit

More than 20 million copies of Michael Jackson's *Thriller* album were sold worldwide in 1984.

You said it!

"Keep a stiff upper lip."
When we're scared, our body reacts. Often the upper lip quivers as we try to keep control of ourselves, to be brave. If you have a stiff upper lip, you're courageous.

What's *that*?!? Centennial

A centennial is the 100th anniversary of a special event. The word comes from *centum,* the Latin word for hundred. In 1984, New Brunswick marked its bicentennial, or 200th birthday (in Latin, *bi-* means "two"), and Toronto celebrated its sesquicentennial, or 150th anniversary (in Latin, *sesqui-* means "one and a half").

JANUARY

Sunday
1

New Year's Day
At the stroke of midnight, Wendy Lim of Toronto and Giovanna Fiore of Montreal become Canada's first New Year's babies of 1984.
☆ **1950** — birth of Philippe Béha, illustrator of *What Do the Fairies Do with All Those Teeth?*

Monday
2

In Landshut, West Germany, the Toronto Young Nationals defeat the Swiss team 7–5 to win the silver medal at the world youth ice hockey tournament.
☆ **1881** — birth of Frederick Varley, Group of Seven painter

Tuesday
3

Let's go! Biwords is a new bilingual game invented in Manitoba. Players use 500 cards to translate words and phrases from one official language to the other. *Allons-y!*
☆ **1939** — birth of Bobby Hull, hockey player

Wednesday
4

New subway lines, a stadium and a swimming pool are being built in Seoul, Korea, for the XXIV Olympiad in the summer of 1988.
☆ **1926** — birth of Betty Kennedy, broadcaster and T.V. personality

Thursday
5

In Oakfield, Nova Scotia, a hairdryer helps resuscitate a frozen newborn Scotch terrier named Pupsicle after he was accidentally left outside overnight.
☆ **1829** — birth of William Christie, biscuit maker

Friday
6

The world's first test-tube quadruplets, all healthy boys, are born in Melbourne, Australia.

Saturday
7

Victor Davis of Waterloo, Ontario, captures the gold medal in the 200-m breaststroke competition at the U.S. Swimming International meet in Austin, Texas.
☆ **1924** — birth of Roloff Beny, painter and photographer

Sunday
8

The two-day celebration of what would have been Elvis Presley's 49th birthday continues in Niagara Falls, Ontario, sponsored by the Elvis in Canada Fan Club.
☆ **1955** — birth of Dave Hodge, sports announcer

Monday
9

People visiting Fredericton, New Brunswick, still gasp in awe when they see the 19-kg stuffed frog at the York-Sunbury Historical Society Museum. It's been on view since it croaked, er, died, nearly 100 years ago.
☆ **1963** — birth of Larry Cain, Olympic canoeist

Tuesday
10

Pop singer Michael Jackson sets a new record with 12 nominations for the annual Grammy Awards.
☆ **1935** — birth of "Rompin' Ronnie" Hawkins, singer-songwriter

JANUARY

Wednesday 11

Richard Nerysoo, a Dene Indian from Fort McPherson, becomes executive leader of the Northwest Territory's government. Nerysoo is the first Native person to hold the post, the highest elected position in the territory.

☆ 1815 — birth of John A. Macdonald, first prime minister of Canada

☆ 1934 — birth of Jean Chrétien, 20th prime minister of Canada

Thursday 12

Tennis pro Carling Bassett, 16, receives the Canadian Press award as Canada's outstanding female athlete of 1983. Wayne Gretzky wins the male athlete award.

☆ 1930 — birth of Tim Horton, hockey player and doughnut king

Friday 13

Prime Minister Pierre Trudeau names outgoing Governor General Ed Schreyer as Canada's high commissioner to Australia.

Saturday 14

In Washington, DC, Kermit the Frog is named honorary chairperson of the 1984 U.S. National Wildlife Week. Kermit will appear with Fozzie Bear in T.V. spots with the theme "Water — we can't live without it!"

☆ 1925 — birth of Louis Quilico, opera singer

Sunday 15

American author Helen Santmyer, 88, took 50 years to complete her new 1344-page novel, ... *And Ladies of the Club*, based on her memories of Waynesboro, Ohio.

☆ 1879 — birth of Mazo de la Roche, author of the Jalna novels

Monday 16

More than 1000 merganser ducks, confused by dense fog, are swept over the Horseshoe Falls at Niagara. Rescuers repair the ducks' broken wings.

☆ 1874 — birth of Robert Service, poet of the Yukon

Tuesday 17

Ski jumper Horst Bulau, winner of seven World Cup events in the 1982–83 season, is named the top amateur athlete in Ontario and receives a sculpture as a prize.

☆ 1929 — birth of Jacques Plante, hockey goaltender and the first goalie to wear a protective mask regularly

Wednesday 18

Daniel Rey and Jean-François Deschenes, grade 13 students in Ottawa, are named winners of a national competititon to put a student-designed experiment on an October flight of the U.S. space shuttle. The students devised a system that can make high-quality mirrors for satellite telescopes while in space.

☆ 1961 — birth of Mark Messier, hockey player

Thursday 19

"Canuckonaut" Dr. Ken Money answers questions about space at a North York, Ontario, school. The most popular question? "How do you pee in space?"

☆ 1934 — birth of Lloyd Robertson, T.V. anchor and reporter

Friday 20

Montrealer Jerry Kobalenko prepares to ski and snowshoe 600 km across northern Labrador. He's packing gourmet *and* survival food on his two sleds.

☆ 1941 — birth of Pierre Lalonde, singer and T.V. host

JANUARY

Saturday 21

Springboard diver Sylvie Bernier, 19, of Ste.-Foy, Quebec, wins the 3-m competition at the Olympium in Etobicoke, Ontario.
☆ **1937** — birth of Jim Unger, cartoonist and creator of "Herman"

Sunday 22

It's Super Bowl XVIII. Football fans watch the Los Angeles Raiders defeat the Washington Redskins 38–9 in Tampa, Florida.

Monday 23

In Florida, Lucky the sea turtle loses one of her $35 000 artificial front flippers, just six days after they were attached in a four-hour, unprecedented operation.
☆ **1929** — birth of John Polanyi, Nobel Prize co-winner in chemistry

Tuesday 24

Kids under 12 are flocking to Chuck E. Cheese outlets for games, pizza, balloons, cake — and plenty of ear-splitting noise, just for parents!
☆ **1955** — birth of Véronique Béliveau, singer and actor

Wednesday 25

Prime Minister Pierre Trudeau, accompanied by his ten-year-old son, Sasha, arrives in Prague, Czechoslovakia, to begin an eight-day tour promoting disarmament.
☆ **1959** — birth of Nicola Morgan, illustrator of *Louis and the Night Sky*

Thursday 26

Ontarians Alex Baumann, Victor Davis and Anne Ottenbrite set new Canadian and world records at the Canadian Winter Nationals short-course swimming championships in Winnipeg, Manitoba.
☆ **1961** — birth of Wayne Gretzky, hockey player

Friday 27

The world's media rush to Los Angeles: Michael Jackson has been taken to the hospital after receiving scalp burns while filming a television commercial.

Saturday 28

Lucky the sea turtle has two front flippers again, thanks to more surgery in Florida. The artificial flipper she lost recently has been reattached.
☆ **1822** — birth of Alexander Mackenzie, second prime minister of Canada

Sunday 29

Hollywood heart-throb Mel Gibson is in Toronto to film *Mrs. Soffel*, also starring Diane Keaton.

Monday 30

Sasha Trudeau and his father, Pierre, arrive in East Berlin, East Germany, for peace talks with local dignitaries.
☆ **1915** — birth of John Ireland, actor

Tuesday 31

It's no yolk! Some Canadian high school students are learning parenting skills — by taking care of a raw egg "child."
☆ **1965** — birth of Ofra Harnoy, cellist

FEBRUARY

Extra! Extra!

The Sarajevo Olympics

Fifteen thousand athletes from around the world have gathered in Sarajevo, Yugoslavia, for the Winter Olympic Games. Speed skater Gaëtan Boucher of Quebec carried Canada's flag at the opening ceremonies at Zetra Stadium. A record 49 nations will compete at the Games, including six countries that sent one-person teams. It's a mystery how Erroll Frazier of the Virgin Islands practised speed skating, or how George Tucker of Puerto Rico found enough snow to luge along!

Beautiful Barbie Is 25

Barbie, the dress-up doll known all over the world, is 25 years old. "Born" in 1959, Barbie cost only $3 when she first appeared on store shelves. Millions of dolls later, there have been Barbie dolls with hair that grows and can be dyed; kissing Barbies; Ken, Barbie's boyfriend; and her close pal, Skipper. Tiffany and Co. has made a silver replica of Barbie to celebrate her silver anniversary.

Trivia tidbit

North Americans had more than 3000 Valentine's Day card designs to choose from in 1984, ranging from traditional hearts to joggers asking, "Your pace or mine?"

What's *that*?!? Epicentre

When an earthquake occurs, its epicentre is the part of the earth's surface that is directly above the source of the quake.

You said it!

"Strike while the iron is hot." Blacksmiths heat metal until it is soft enough to be formed into a desired shape. They have to hammer, or strike, the iron quickly, before it hardens and is no longer pliable. Similarly, you have to approach someone when you think the time is right.

Wednesday 1
Not enough homework? Students at the University of British Columbia put a Volkswagen Beetle on top of a 17-storey clock tower.
☆ 1882 — birth of Louis St. Laurent, 12th prime minister of Canada

Thursday 2
Chinese New Year / Groundhog Day
Inexpensive copies of famous brand-name wristwatches, such as Cartier and Rolex, are causing a fashion fuss at street stalls across Canada.

Friday 3
Ottawa biochemist Ken Storey has discovered that frogs are the only vertebrates that can be completely frozen and not die.

FEBRUARY

Saturday
4
Breakdancing is the latest teen fad. Masters of this acrobatic style of dance perform moves with names like "scissors" and "helicopter swipes."

Sunday
5
Canadians take gold medals in all three men's categories at the fourth Canada Cup international judo championships in Montreal.

Monday
6
Tom Selleck, star of *Magnum P.I.*, is television's heart-throb of the moment — as a result, moustaches and Selleck-look-alike contests are popular.
☆ 1946 — birth of Kate McGarrigle, singer-songwriter

Tuesday
7
American astronaut Bruce McCandless, wearing a jet-powered backpack, steps from the shuttle *Challenger* to become the first person to fly freely through space.
☆ 1968 — birth of Mark Tewksbury, Olympic swimmer

Wednesday
8
The Winter Olympics open in the resort city of Sarajevo, Yugoslavia. Officials predict that more than one billion fans will tune in to the Games on television.

Thursday
9
In St. John's, Newfoundland, the federal government has launched a five-year campaign to convince beefeaters to try some fish. Holy mackerel!
☆ 1894 — birth of Billy Bishop, World War I pilot

Friday
10
Gaëtan Boucher of Quebec, wins an Olympic bronze medal in the 500-m speed skating competition.

Saturday
11
Residents of southern Alberta and British Columbia feel an earthquake measuring 4.6 on the Richter scale. The epicentre is southeast of Lethbridge.
☆ 1947 — birth of Abby Hoffman, middle-distance runner

Sunday
12
Eddie Burt, 11, of Kootenay, BC, and 12 other Canadians begin a five-month international tour promoting world peace.

Monday
13
In Moscow, Konstantin Chernenko is named the new general secretary of the Soviet Communist Party.

Tuesday
14
Valentine's Day ♥
Gaëtan Boucher wins the 1000-m speed skating event and collects Canada's first Olympic gold medal in Sarajevo.
☆ 1935 — birth of Rob McConnell, trombonist and composer

Wednesday
15
People are dusting off their fondue pots and dipping all kinds of edibles into warm melted cheese or chocolate.

Thursday
16
It's Boucher again! The Quebec speed skater becomes the first Canadian to win three medals (two of them gold) at a Winter Olympics. Brian Orser wins silver in the men's singles figure-skating competition.
☆ 1953 — birth of Lanny McDonald, hockey player

Friday
17
The six finalists in the Canadian astronaut program pose for photos in Ottawa. Roberta Bondar, Marc Garneau, Steve MacLean, Ken Money, Bob Thirsk and Bjarni Tryggvason were selected from thousands of applicants.
☆ 1938 — birth of Martha Henry, actor

FEBRUARY

Saturday
18
In Toronto, ballet great Mikhail Baryshnikov performs with the National Ballet of Canada.
☆ **1933** — birth of László Gál, illustrator of *The Twelve Dancing Princesses*

Sunday
19
A ceremony on ice in Sarajevo's Zetra Arena brings the Winter Olympics to a close. Calgary, Alberta, will host the next Winter Olympics, in 1988.

Monday
20
Regina, Saskatchewan, is the site of the first Hole-ympics. Competitors push old outhouses around frozen Wascana Lake.
☆ **1942** — birth of Phil Esposito, hockey player

Tuesday
21
Yi Li Fast Food, in Peking, is almost ready to open. It will be the first Western-style fast food restaurant in China and will serve hamburgers, hot dogs, salted duck eggs and soybean snacks.
☆ **1963** — birth of Lori Fung, Olympic gymnast

Wednesday
22
David, the world-famous 12-year-old boy who lived in a plastic bubble to protect him from infection, dies after only two weeks outside his sterile environment.
☆ **1948** — birth of Paul Kropp, author of *Cottage Crazy*

Thursday
23
A brilliant blue-green meteor over Alberta causes fear and excitement. Telephone calls flood newspaper offices and televison and police stations.
☆ **1949** — birth of Marc Garneau, first Canadian astronaut to go into space

Friday
24
Nick Soriano of Toronto spends his workdays surrounded by naked bodies — mannequins, that is. His company makes and imports up to 5000 of them each year, in all shapes, sexes and ages.
☆ **1932** — birth of John Vernon, actor

Saturday
25
The Saskatchewan government recently bought the 1885 Batoche diary of Métis leader Louis Riel. The important historical document is being restored by the provincial archives.
☆ **1752** — birth of John Graves Simcoe, lieutenant governor of Upper Canada

Sunday
26
Last year, American Samantha Smith, 12, wrote to Soviet leader Yuri Andropov about her fears of nuclear war. He invited her to the Soviet Union for a visit. Now she's on T.V. interviewing presidential candidates for the U.S. election!
☆ **1928** — birth of Monique Leyrac, singer and actor

Monday
27
Ken Danby has completed a set of sports paintings showing Canada's athletes competing at this year's Winter Olympics. The watercolours will be auctioned and the funds donated to the Olympic Trust.
☆ **1899** — birth of Charles Best, co-discoverer of insulin

Tuesday
28
Steve Podborski, the last of a group of downhill skiers known as the "Crazy Canucks," announces his upcoming retirement. "It's time for a change."
☆ **1961** — birth of René Simard, singer

Wednesday
29
Prime Minister Pierre Trudeau announces his retirement after 16 years in office.
☆ **1936** — birth of Henri "the Pocket Rocket" Richard, hockey player

MARCH

Extra! Extra!

The Halfpenny "Disappears"

The copper coin called the halfpenny (pronounced hay-penny) has been British coinage since King Edward I introduced it 704 years ago. But inflation has made it nearly useless, and it now costs more to mint than its face value of about 0.8 cents. This month, the Royal Mint will stop making the coin.

100 Years Old in 1984

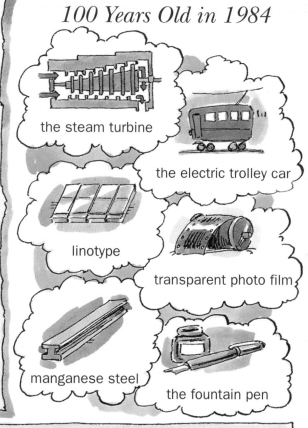

the steam turbine

the electric trolley car

linotype

transparent photo film

manganese steel

the fountain pen

Trivia tidbit

In 1984, North Americans ate an average of 2.1 kg of potato chips each.

You said it!

"You've got something up your sleeve!" Many magicians perform a trick where something, such as a scarf, is hidden up a sleeve and then suddenly made to appear as though from thin air. The expression means you're hiding something, or you're about to surprise someone.

What's *that*?!? Cajun

In 1604, the first French immigrants to Canada settled in Acadia, a colony that included Nova Scotia and New Brunswick. The Acadians were banished from their lands by the British in 1755, and settled in the United States. The term "Cajun" is a corruption of "Acadian" and usually identifies the Acadian descendants now living in Louisiana.

MARCH

Thursday 1
Sailor styles, including middy shirts, nautical stripes and lots of navy blue, are back in fashion.
☆ 1947 — birth of Alan Thicke, actor

Friday 2
To raise funds for charity, Mark Sutton of Victoria plans to spend the next 13 months and 10 days in his tent — perched on a flagpole!
☆ 1942 — birth of Luc Plamondon, composer-songwriter

Saturday 3
At Charlottetown, Prince Edward Island, the Manitoba squad wins the Canadian women's curling championship with a 5–4 victory over Nova Scotia.
☆ 1847 — birth of Alexander Graham Bell, inventor of the telephone

Sunday 4
Gaëtan Boucher continues his winning streak, this time in Trondheim, Norway, where the speed skater wins the world sprint championships.
☆ 1949 — birth of Carroll Baker, singer-songwriter

Monday 5
Happy 150th! Toronto celebrates its sesquicentennial with a party for thousands at Nathan Phillips Square. On the menu: 19 000 slices of cake and 7000 cups of cocoa.
☆ 1883 — birth of Charles Barbeau, folklorist

Tuesday 6
Winnipeg's Ukrainian Shumka Dancers mark their 25th anniversary with a six-city cross-Canada tour.
☆ 1940 — birth of Ken Danby, artist

Wednesday 7
Kathleen Leggett, an 18-year-old science student at the University of Toronto, is praised for her help in finding a key mechanism in the body's immune system.
☆ 1951 — birth of Diane Jones Konihowski, Olympic pentathlete

Thursday 8
International Women's Day
More than 1500 horses can be found at the Toronto CNE Coliseum for Quarterama, the second largest quarter-horse show in North America.
☆ 1896 — birth of Charlotte Whitton, Canada's first woman mayor (of Ottawa)

Friday 9
One thousand Gaëtan Boucher fans gather at Mirabel International Airport in Montreal to greet their homecoming hero with cheers and banners.
☆ 1934 — birth of Marlene Stewart Streit, champion golfer

Saturday 10
Mountain climber Roger Marshall of Golden, BC, has been given permission by the Chinese authorities to complete a solo journey up Mount Everest, the world's highest mountain, in 1986.
☆ 1947 — birth of Kim Campbell, 19th and first woman prime minister of Canada

MARCH

Sunday
11
On Whistler Mountain in British Columbia, Steve Podborski ends his ten-year downhill skiing career with a fifth-place finish in the World Cup event.
☆ **1930** — birth of Claude Jutra, film maker

Monday
12
Splash, starring Tom Hanks and Canadians John Candy and Eugene Levy, is a huge comedy hit in movie theatres across North America.
☆ **1821** — birth of Sir John Abbott, third prime minister of Canada

Tuesday
13
The Canadian board game Trivial Pursuit is expected to sell 30 million copies in 1984. It takes 68 million kilograms of paper each year to make the games.
☆ **1973** — birth of Allison Higson, champion swimmer

Wednesday
14
Quebec City native Marc Garneau is chosen as the first Canadian to go into space. In October, he'll join five U.S. astronauts on the space shuttle *Discovery*.
☆ **1968** — birth of Megan Follows, actor

Thursday
15
Canada Post issues a new stamp to commemorate the founding of Yellowknife, NWT, in 1934.
☆ **1943** — birth of David Cronenberg, film maker

Friday
16
King Juan Carlos and Queen Sofia of Spain are in Canada for a seven-day tour.
☆ **1951** — birth of Kate Nelligan, actor

Saturday
17
St. Patrick's Day
Smokey the Bear, one of North America's most famous animal characters, is celebrating his 40th birthday. Smokey's got a new logo, but his message remains the same: "Remember, only *you* can prevent forest fires."
☆ **1937** — birth of Aqjangajuk Shaa, stone carver

Sunday
18
Archaeologists believe a mysterious circle of stones found at Tipperary Creek, Saskatchewan, is a medicine wheel or a calendar, constructed within the last 1500 years.
☆ **1871** — birth of Frederick Coburn, artist

Monday
19
Sports equipment stores can't keep up with the demand for BMX and motocross bikes. There are even kits available to make an old bicycle *look* like a BMX.
☆ **1942** — birth of Sonia Craddock, author of *Hal, the Third Class Hero*

Tuesday
20
Cajun cookin' is H-O-T! There's gumbo, jambalaya, crayfish, okra and plenty of hot sauce. Pass the water, please!
☆ **1939** — birth of Brian Mulroney, 18th prime minister of Canada

Wednesday
21
It's the Canadian film world's big night. Genie Awards go to *The Terry Fox Story* (Best Motion Picture), Eric Fryer (Best Actor) and Martha Henry (Best Actress).
☆ **1904** — birth of Jehane Benoît, cooking expert and media personality

MARCH

Thursday 22
The current best-selling recordings include the soundtracks from the movies *The Big Chill* and *Footloose*, and albums by Hall & Oates, Lionel Richie and Billy Idol.
☆ **1972** — birth of Elvis Stojko, Olympic figure skater

Friday 23
A new stamp marks the founding of the Montreal Symphony Orchestra 50 years ago *and* commemorates 1984 as the Year of the Arts.
☆ **1910** — birth of Harry Welsh, physicist

Saturday 24
Michael Douglas and Kathleen Turner are thrilling movie audiences with the box-office hit *Romancing the Stone.*
☆ **1890** — birth of Agnes Macphail, first woman elected to Canada's Parliament

Sunday 25
In Spruce Grove, Alberta, the home team beats Quebec 5–4 in overtime to win the Canadian women's hockey championship.
☆ **1931** — birth of Jack Chambers, painter

Monday 26
A farmer in Virginia has invented an automatic pancake machine that produces 60 flapjacks every three minutes.
☆ **1963** — birth of Roch Voisine, singer-songwriter

Tuesday 27
Twelve Canadian climbers are preparing for a future expedition they're calling "Everest Light." Only the bare necessities will be taken up Mount Everest, and no Sherpa guides will go with the group.
☆ **1952** — birth of Richard and Marie-Claire Séguin, twin singer-songwriters

Wednesday 28
The sap is running, and the maple sugaring process in southern Ontario, Quebec and the Maritimes has begun. Sugaring-off parties will be held after the last kettle of sap has been boiled down.
☆ **1951** — birth of Karen Kain, dancer

Thursday 29
Students at the Arthur Pechey School in Prince Albert, Saskatchewan, have discovered a new use for an old bathtub. They sit and read in a pillow-lined, claw-foot version in the school library.
☆ **1956** — birth of Ted Staunton, author of *Anna Takes Charge*

Friday 30
A special dinner is held at the Canadian Forces Command & Staff College in Toronto to celebrate the 60th anniversary of the Royal Canadian Air Force.
☆ **1968** — birth of Céline Dion, singer

Saturday 31
Runner Steve Fonyo dips his artificial leg in the Atlantic, off St. John's, Newfoundland, and begins his Journey for Lives run across Canada to raise money for cancer research.
☆ **1928** — birth of Gordie Howe, hockey player

APRIL

Extra! Extra!

Boy George Is Everywhere!

In private life he's George O'Dowd, but to his millions of fans he's pop phenomenon Boy George. He and his band, Culture Club, have performed their hit song "Karma Chameleon" across North America. Boy George is so popular, he's created new fashion fads with his long hair, dramatic make-up, and neon vests layered over skirts and robes.

Academy Award Winners

Millions of viewers around the world watched the film industry celebrate Oscar Night, the evening of the Academy Awards. The major awards were:

☆ Best Actor — Robert Duvall, in *Tender Mercies*

☆ Best Actress — Shirley MacLaine, in *Terms of Endearment*

☆ Best Picture — *Terms of Endearment*

Trivia tidbit

According to United Nations statistics, the world population in 1984 was 4.67 billion people.

You said it!

"Go back to the drawing board." When an architect or engineer designs something, she usually sits at her drawing board, or drafting table, to make blueprints, or detailed plans. If the plans fail, it's time for her to go back to her board, start over, and re-draw the plans.

What's *that*?!? The *Titanic*

The *Titanic* was a luxury ocean liner advertised as "unsinkable." On its first, or maiden, voyage in 1912, more than 1500 people died when the *Titanic* sank off Newfoundland. At first it was believed the liner sank after hitting an iceberg; however, more research points to poor construction as the cause of the tragedy.

Sunday
1
April Fool's Day
Friendships are tested as pranksters across Canada play practical jokes on their pals. Just kidding?!
☆ 1931 — birth of Cliff Lumsdon, long-distance swimmer

Monday
2
A professor at the University of Massachusetts has developed a "fishfurter." It's reportedly shaped like a hot dog, is low-fat, and has no fishy taste or smell.

Tuesday
3
Rakesh Sharma becomes India's first space traveller as he goes into orbit with two Soviet cosmonauts on *Soyuz T-11*. He'll try to use yoga to combat space sickness.
☆ 1918 — birth of Louis Applebaum, composer-conductor

APRIL

Wednesday 4
Statistics Canada reports that Saskatchewan has become the sixth province to reach a population of one million.
☆ 1952 — birth of Karen Magnussen, figure skater

Thursday 5
In Victoria, Mark Sutton is 36 days closer to his goal — the new world record for pole-sitting. Only 368 days to go!

Friday 6
The World's Biggest Daffodil Parade, down Yonge Street in Toronto, kicks off the Canadian Cancer Society's annual campaign for research funds.

Saturday 7
The musical version of Mordecai Richler's novel *The Apprenticeship of Duddy Kravitz* premieres at Edmonton's Citadel Theatre.
☆ 1908 — birth of Percy Faith, composer

Sunday 8
Prem Tinsulanonda, the prime minister of Thailand, arrives in Vancouver to begin a 20-day, six-country tour.
☆ 1924 — birth of Frederic Back, Oscar-winning animated-film maker

Monday 9
Canada's National Film Board wins two Oscars, for *Boys and Girls* (Best Live Action Short Film) and *Flamenco at 5:15* (Best Documentary Short Subject).

Tuesday 10
Callers can now pay with credit cards instead of coins, using the new charge-a-call system operating in some telephone booths.

Wednesday 11
Residents of Baie Comeau, Quebec, feel tremors of an earthquake. Tremors have become a regular event here; there's at least one such quake each year.

Thursday 12
Tonight, Canadian impressionist and comedian Jim Carrey makes his first appearance as the star of *The Duck Factory*, a new television sit-com.

Friday 13
The Australian cabinet votes unanimously to replace "God Save the Queen" with "Advance Australia Fair" as the country's new national anthem.
☆ 1861 — birth of Margaret Marshall Saunders, author of *Beautiful Joe*

Saturday 14
Natasha and Tabitha, two lowland gorillas living at the Metropolitan Toronto Zoo, are preparing for their move to the Calgary Zoo in search of mates.
☆ 1918 — birth of Scott Young, author of *Boy on Defence*

Sunday 15
The U.S. Coast Guard, on behalf of the Titanic Memorial Society, places a wreath on the ocean off Newfoundland, near where the luxury liner sank 72 years ago.

Monday 16
Passover
Three-time Canadian women's figure skating champion Kay Thompson has signed a multi-year professional contract with Ice Capades.
☆ 1949 — birth of Sandy Hawley, jockey

Tuesday 17
The makers of Cabbage Patch dolls announce their new products: Preemies, pets called Koosas, and everything from tricycles to sleeping bags with Cabbage Patch designs.
☆ 1949 — birth of Martyn Godfrey, author of *Mall Rats*

APRIL

Wednesday 18
An English couple using a single parachute jumps 276 m from the top of the Eiffel Tower in Paris. The last successful, but illegal, jump was made in 1911.
☆ **1953** — birth of Rick Moranis, actor

Thursday 19
Saskatchewan-born Brian Dickson is sworn in as chief justice of the Supreme Court of Canada.

Friday 20
Solemn Toronto crowds gather to watch the annual Good Friday procession through the streets near St. Francis of Assissi Church.
☆ **1949** — birth of Toller Cranston, figure skater and artist

Saturday 21
Lucy Philpott of Vancouver can hear for the first time in two years, with the help of a microchip implant in her ear. She's the first Canadian to receive the device.

Sunday 22
Easter
The tattooed arm of Hell's Angel "Gus" Christie will carry the Summer Olympic torch for one kilometre of its journey into Los Angeles this summer. The Hell's Angels motorcycle club has paid, like other organizations, to sponsor a runner.

Monday 23
A 20-kg chocolate Easter Bunny has been stolen from a California store. The store owners have posted a reward of 2.5 kg of jelly beans for its safe return.
☆ **1897** — birth of Lester Pearson, 14th prime minister of Canada

Tuesday 24
Teens are buying the albums and imitating the hair styles of Cyndi Lauper, the Thompson Twins and Ozzy Osbourne.

Wednesday 25
At 231 cm, Sandy Allen is already the world's tallest woman. Special shoes being made for her to correct a leg-length problem will allow her to walk fully upright — and make her 5 cm taller.
☆ **1904** — birth of Paul-Emile Léger, cardinal and missionary

Thursday 26
For the first time in its 80-year history, the Empire Club of Canada elects a woman president, Catherine Charlton.
☆ **1948** — birth of Alfred Sung, fashion designer

Friday 27
In Toronto, costumed "soldiers" re-stage the Battle of York (fought in 1813) as part of the city's sesquicentennial celebrations.

Saturday 28
Tens of thousands of singing demonstrators parade through the streets of downtown Vancouver in the fourth annual Walk for Peace.
☆ **1946** — birth of Ginette Reno, singer

Sunday 29
Steel scaffolding is gradually covering the Statue of Liberty in New York Harbor. A $30-million renovation will restore the statue to its original condition in time for Liberty's 100th birthday in 1986.
☆ **1918** — birth of Aser Rothstein, research physiologist

Monday 30
Athletes and sports "builders" George Reed, Leslie Cliff, Harry "Red" Foster, Pat Ramage and Gaëtan Boucher are elected to the Canadian Sports Hall of Fame.
☆ **1951** — birth of Ken Whiteley, singer-musician

Extra! Extra!

Another "First" for Jeanne Sauvé

In May 1984, Jeanne Sauvé became Canada's first woman governor general and moved into Ottawa's Rideau Hall to begin her mission for peace and national unity. Born in Prud'homme, Saskatchewan, in 1922, Mme. Sauvé was the first woman Speaker of the House of Commons. She was also one of the first women elected to Parliament from Quebec.

…*But* two *gloves make a pair!*

In 1984, thousands of Canadian Michael Jackson fans imitated their pop idol by wearing one glove. On tour this year, Jackson's right hand was always covered with a sparkling white glove, and manufacturers soon copied the accessory. A huge newspaper advertisement for a Toronto department store said, "Beat It down to Simpsons for 'the Glitter Glove.'" Only $5.99 for *one* non-washable glove of gold- or silver-tone glitter on white cotton.

Trivia tidbit

In 1984, more than 400 000 Canadian high school students created science fair projects.

What's *that*?!? *Magna Carta*

The *Magna Carta* (Latin for "great charter") was a document signed by King John in the year 1215 at Runnymede, England, to avoid an uprising of the country's nobles against him. The document recorded the relationship between the king and his subjects, and is considered the basis of other charters of civil rights in countries around the world.

You said it!

"I'll give him thumbs down."
In ancient Rome, the crowds attending gladiator contests decided the fate of the competitors. If a spectator thought the gladiator fought valiantly, he made two fists and extended his thumbs up, meaning "well done." If the contestant fought poorly, the sign was reversed to "thumbs down," a sign of rejection. Thumbs down usually meant death to the gladiator. The expressions, and the gestures, are still signs of approval or dislike.

MAY

Tuesday
1
In Toronto, the Art Gallery of Ontario opens a show featuring 16 abstract portraits of Canada's prime ministers by painter William Ronald.
☆ **1916** — birth of Glenn Ford, actor

Wednesday
2
Haligonians Garry Sowerby and Ken Langley celebrate after reaching Nordkapp, Norway. The two drove through desert heat, ambushes and heavy snow, from the bottom of Africa to the top of Norway in a record 28 days, 12 hours and 10 minutes.
☆ **1920** — birth of William Hutt, actor

Thursday
3
A rancher in La Rivière, Manitoba, has been told his cows have bad breath. He says it's caused by a weed in the hay they eat, but bad breath or not, they're still good cows!
☆ **1913** — birth of Joyce Barkhouse, author of *Anna's Pet*

Friday
4
The *Argo*, a reconstruction of a Bronze Age ship, sets sail from Greece on a voyage of 3000 nautical miles to test the legend of Jason and the quest for the Golden Fleece.
☆ **1928** — birth of Maynard Ferguson, jazz trumpeter

Saturday
5
Disney's Donald Duck is 50 years old this year. Celebration plans include a parade at Walt Disney World that will feature 50 real ducks waddling behind the birthday boy, er, duck.
☆ **1843** — birth of William Beers, who campaigned to have lacrosse accepted as Canada's national game

Sunday
6
There's a media blitz going on for Harrison Ford's return in *Indiana Jones and the Temple of Doom*, due for release later this month. Look out, Indie!
☆ **1849** — birth of Wyatt Eaton, painter

Monday
7
In Olympia, Greece, an actor dressed as an ancient Greek priestess officially lights the torch that will travel to the Summer Olympic Games in Los Angeles, California.

Tuesday
8
Buddhists around the world celebrate the 2528th birthday of Lord Buddha.
☆ **1912** — birth of George Woodcock, writer and historian

Wednesday
9
In Toronto, ballet great Rudolf Nureyev guest stars with Karen Kain and the National Ballet of Canada in his production of *Sleeping Beauty*.
☆ **1909** — birth of Don Messer, fiddler and T.V. host

Thursday
10
A new U.S. company offers a service called SpaceShot. For $5, they'll blast any message of 25 words or less into outer space via transmitters and complex computers.
☆ **1958** — birth of Gaëtan Boucher, Olympic speed skater

MAY

Friday 11
After eight years of planning, Vancouver architect Arthur Erickson's design for the new Canadian embassy in Washington, DC, is unveiled. The completed building is scheduled to open in 1986.
☆ 1927 — birth of Mort Sahl, comedian

Saturday 12
The 1984 World's Fair opens in New Orleans, Louisiana. The site of the six-month-long fair covers 90 000 m² and features the world's largest ferris wheel.
☆ 1921 — birth of Farley Mowat, author of *Lost in the Barrens*

Sunday 13
Steve Fonyo passes the 800-km mark and nears Cape Breton on his cross-Canada Journey for Lives run for cancer research funds.
☆ 1937 — birth of Roch Carrier, author of *The Hockey Sweater*

Monday 14
In Ottawa, jets dip their wings in salute overhead and children's choirs sing as Jeanne Sauvé is sworn in as Canada's 23rd (and first woman) governor general.
☆ 1953 — birth of Tom Cochrane, singer-songwriter

Tuesday 15
British explorer David Hempleman-Adams has become the first person to complete a solo walk to the magnetic North Pole. His gruelling 400-km walk across the Arctic icecap took 22 days.
☆ 1923 — birth of Ronald Thom, architect

Wednesday 16
Postal workers in Montreal release 200 homing pigeons to help mark Post Office Employees' Week. The birds, adopted as the week's symbol, headed home to St.-Hyacinthe, Quebec, 48 km away.
☆ 1873 — birth of Charles Noble, inventor

Thursday 17
Canada's first test-tube twins, Sean and Ian, are born at Toronto East General Hospital.
☆ 1944 — birth of Jesse Winchester, singer-songwriter

Friday 18
Scott Hayman and Terry Gerritsen, high school students in Oakville, Ontario, win first place at the Canada-wide Science Fair in Halifax. They translated sound waves into computer-generated graphics.
☆ 1963 — birth of Marty McSorley, hockey player

Saturday 19
It's a sweet victory in Edmonton's Northlands Coliseum as the Oilers win their first ever Stanley Cup, four games to one, over the New York Islanders.
☆ 1817 — birth of Theodore Heintzman, piano maker

Sunday 20
A food preference study says that ice cream tops the list of kids' favourite foods, followed by doughnuts, chocolate chip cookies and french fries. (Eggplant comes in last.)
☆ 1929 — birth of Sydney van den Bergh, astronomer

MAY

Monday
21

Victoria Day
Young boys and girls compete in the saddle at the Little Britches Rodeo in High River, Alberta.

Tuesday
22

A parade through downtown Edmonton celebrates the Oilers' Stanley Cup win over four-time champs, the New York Islanders.
☆ **1622** — birth of Louis de Buade, Comte de Frontenac, governor of New France

Wednesday
23

Smurfs are everywhere! The blue, big-nosed beings can be found in television cartoons and on a wide range of products, such as pyjamas and board games, totalling $1 billion in sales.
☆ **1928** — birth of Pauline Julien, singer-songwriter

Thursday
24

Pope John Paul II names Rev. Leonard Boyle of Toronto as the new head of the Vatican Library, established in the year 1450 and filled with manuscripts dating back to the fourth century.
☆ **1902** — birth of Lionel Conacher, all-round athlete

Friday
25

One of the four remaining copies of England's Magna Carta is on display at McMaster University in Hamilton, Ontario. The 769-year-old document is the basis of our modern justice system.
☆ **1900** — birth of Malcolm Norris, Métis leader

Saturday
26

The house in Lacombe, Alberta, where former governor general Roland Michener was born in 1900 is opened to the public as a new historical site.
☆ **1919** — birth of Jay Silverheels, actor

Sunday
27

I Am a Hotel, an experimental film based on the songs of Montreal's Leonard Cohen, has taken two top prizes at the Montreux International Festival in Switzerland.
☆ **1914** — birth of Hugh Le Caine, inventor of the first synthesizer

Monday
28

Fifty years ago today, Yvonne, Annette, Cécile, Emilie and Marie Dionne, the world's first surviving quintuplets, were born in Corbeil, Ontario.
☆ **1947** — birth of Lynn Johnston, cartoonist and creator of "For Better or For Worse"

Tuesday
29

Prime Minister Pierre Trudeau announces the appointment of Montreal-born Mr. Justice Gerald Le Dain to the Supreme Court of Canada.
☆ **1955** — birth of Michèle Lemieux, illustrator of *Amahl and the Night Visitors*

Wednesday
30

Kwik Kurlers, the latest trendy hair fad, are pliable foam fibre hair rollers. While they're on your head, the rollers make you look like a space alien — but you get plenty of curls!
☆ **1955** — birth of Christopher House, dancer and choreographer

Thursday
31

Jumping fedoras! *Indiana Jones and the Temple of Doom* is thrilling movie audiences, to the tune of $42 million in only six days since its release.
☆ **1961** — birth of Corey Hart, singer-songwriter

JUNE

Extra! Extra!

Canada Gives U.S. Eagle Chicks

Six bald-eagle chicks have been taken from nests in Cape Breton and flown to Massachusetts to aid the declining eagle population in the United States. Pesticides and hunters have left only about 1600 pairs of eagles in the United States. The young Canadian eagles will be freed into the wild to fend for themselves after three months. Canada also plans to ship ten eaglets from Manitoba to New Jersey, and a dozen more from Saskatchewan to Pennsylvania.

450 Years Later — A Coin

In 1984, a commemorative coin was minted in honour of explorer Jacques Cartier's first voyage to Canada in 1534. Toronto-area artist Hector Greville designed the new dollar coin, which shows Cartier and two of his men claiming the land for France.

Trivia tidbit

You can put 'em on ice cream, in your pancakes, even mix up some of their frozen juice concentrate: in 1984, Atlantic Canada harvested 9 million kilograms of wild blueberries.

What's *that*?!? Caboose

The brightly coloured caboose is the last car on a freight train. It often has a kitchen and sleeping areas for the train's crew and a lookout area on its roof. Its unusual name is believed to come from the Dutch word *kabuis*, whose original meaning has been lost.

You said it!

"He's up in the crow's nest."
A crow's nest is the circular "basket," usually built of wood and located high on a ship's mast, where the birds flew. Sailors climbed the rigging to the nest to scan the horizon for land or other ships. Anyone perched up high on land or sea, and serving as a lookout, is said to be "in the crow's nest."

JUNE

Friday 1
Queen Elizabeth II loans 21 drawings by Leonardo da Vinci to the Art Gallery of Ontario for a two-month show. They're usually "at home" in Windsor Castle's Royal Library.
☆ **1961** — birth of Paul Coffey, hockey player

Saturday 2
Forty-one Tall Ships begin a 1760-km race from Bermuda to Halifax, Nova Scotia.
☆ **1935** — birth of Carol Shields, novelist

Sunday 3
Helen Stratigos, 12, and Carmelina Geremia, 11, have spent the last two years raising money for the World Wildlife Fund. In their hometown of Scarborough, Ontario, the two girls are given a "Superkids" award sponsored by *OWL* magazine and Environment Canada.
☆ **1954** — birth of Dan Hill, singer-songwriter

Monday 4
Train enthusiasts express their unhappiness as Canadian National Railways and Canadian Pacific Rail announce they want to test a modern technology "black box" to replace cabooses.
☆ **1951** — birth of Maryann Kovalski, illustrator of *I Went to the Zoo*

Tuesday 5
There's lots of concern in White Rock, BC, where a 10-m-long grey whale has washed ashore. It's the third dead whale found on the beach in three weeks.
☆ **1939** — birth of Joe Clark, 16th prime minister of Canada

Wednesday 6
Two hundred World War II veterans from Toronto's Queen's Own Rifles parade and pray on the beach at Bernières-sur-Mer, Normandy, France, to mark the 40th anniversary of D-Day.
☆ **1920** — birth of Jan Rubes, actor and singer

Thursday 7
Marc-André Hamelin of Montreal and David Swan of Saskatoon are among the 20 pianists continuing in the elimination rounds of the 17th Montreal International Music Competition.
☆ **1929** — birth of John Turner, 17th prime minister of Canada

Friday 8
More than 100 of the world's best photojournalists photograph Canada from sea to sea today in a 24-hour project. The photos will illustrate a book called *A Day in the Life of Canada*.
☆ **1912** — birth of Clyde Gilmour, broadcaster

Saturday 9
The 13th Canadian Open Frisbee Disc Championships fill the air at Centre Island, Toronto, with colourful, fast-flying, plastic discs.
☆ **1882** — birth of Angus Walters, skipper of the *Bluenose*

Sunday 10
Summer movies *Ghostbusters,* starring Canadian Rick Moranis, and *Gremlins* are leaving audiences screaming — with laughter *and* fear.

JUNE

Monday 11

The original Batmobile from the popular 1960s T.V. series has been auctioned for $64 000. Also sold: Robin's Batcycle and a car trimmed in 24-karat gold and owned by Elvis.
☆ 1945 — birth of Robert Munsch, author of *Wait and See*

Tuesday 12

Anchors aweigh! In Halifax, "Tall Ships fever" goes to Rose Turton's head — literally! She has her long hair fashioned into a hairy model of the *Bluenose*.
☆ 1959 — birth of Steve Bauer, Olympic cyclist

Wednesday 13

More Canadians in showbiz: Howie Mandel is the cartoon voice of Gizmo, of T.V.'s *Gremlins* fame, and Martin Short has joined the cast of *Saturday Night Live*.
☆ 1924 — birth of Harold Town, artist

Thursday 14

Paul Anka sings "My Way," and Prime Minister Pierre Trudeau, joined on stage by his three sons, says farewell to 10 000 Liberal delegates, journalists and friends at the Ottawa Civic Centre. His 22-minute speech is his last major one while in office.
☆ 1924 — birth of Arthur Erickson, architect

Friday 15

Doc and Sleepy, male and female Peking ducks, are given to Toronto's Metro Zoo by Walt Disney Productions in honour of Donald Duck's 50th birthday. A Peking duck was Walt Disney's model for Donald.
☆ 1789 — birth of Josiah Henson, founder of an Ontario community for fugitive slaves

Saturday 16

John Turner wins the Liberal Party leadership race in Ottawa and will replace Trudeau as Canada's next prime minister.
☆ 1874 — birth of Arthur Meighen, ninth prime minister of Canada

Sunday 17

Alex Baumann sets a new world record in the 400-m individual medley at the Esso Cup Olympic swimming trials in Etobicoke, Ontario.
☆ 1930 — birth of Rosemary Brown, social activist

Monday 18

In Fredericton, parades, cakes and musicals mark the 200th anniversary of the day in 1784 when King George III of England signed a document that created the province known as New Brunswick.
☆ 1966 — birth of Kurt Browning, world champion figure skater

Tuesday 19

John Mackie ends a 16-day canoe trip from Scarborough, Ontario, to Montreal. He followed a route taken by the explorer René-Robert Cavalier, Sieur de La Salle, 300 years ago, but he travelled in the opposite direction!
☆ 1902 — birth of Guy Lombardo, conductor and musician

Wednesday 20

A new coral-coloured rose has been cultivated to mark Pope John Paul II's visit to Canada this autumn, and 30 bushes of the new species have already been planted in the Vatican garden. A silk replica of the John Paul II Rose is the first approved, official souvenir.
☆ 1857 — birth of Sir Adam Beck, founder of Ontario Hydro

JUNE

Thursday 21
The National Film Board has documented the life of Pete Standing Alone, an Alberta Blood Indian, in the television special "Standing Alone," which premieres tonight.
☆ **1900** — birth of Edward Rogers, broadcasting pioneer

Friday 22
Jeanne Sauvé awards Brigitte Boudreault, 14, of Sept-Îles, Quebec, with the Star of Courage. Brigitte saved a young girl from drowning in a river in 1982.
☆ **1867** — birth of John Pearson, co-designer in 1916 of Canada's new Parliament Buildings

Saturday 23
The skies are filled with 4000 racing pigeons competing in the Upper Canada National race from Fraserdale, Ontario — to wherever each pigeon calls home. The winner is the bird that travels the most metres per minute from the beginning to the end of the race.
☆ **1883** — birth of Frederick "Cyclone" Taylor, first star hockey player

Sunday 24
La Fête National
Edmonton's Violet Archer is honoured with the Composer of the Year award in Toronto by the Canadian Music Council.

Monday 25
Contestants from various Toronto media begin the Great Toronto (England)-to-Toronto (Canada) Race, in honour of the Ontario city's sesquicentennial. There will be prizes for speed and originality.
☆ **1952** — birth of Tololwa Mollel, author of *The King and the Tortoise*

Tuesday 26
Stuntman Terry McGauran rides his motorcycle up the CN Tower's 1760 stairs to mark the tower's eighth birthday. The feat will be recorded in the *Guinness World Book of Records*.
☆ **1854** — birth of Sir Robert Borden, eighth prime minister of Canada

Wednesday 27
Prime Minister Pierre Trudeau wins the Albert Einstein Peace Prize for his campaign in 17 countries for weapons disarmament. Trudeau has also been nominated for the Nobel Peace Prize.
☆ **1942** — birth of Frank Mills, musician and composer

Thursday 28
Canadian pop group Parachute Club arrives in Cologne, West Germany, to tape a segment of *Montages Markdt*, the country's top pop T.V. show.
☆ **1937** — birth of George Knudson, golfer

Friday 29
With his formal resignation in the hands of Governor General Jeanne Sauvé, Pierre Trudeau steps down from the office of prime minister.
☆ **1944** — birth of Charlie Watt, Inuit senator

Saturday 30
In Ottawa, John Turner is sworn in as Canada's 17th prime minister.
☆ **1948** — birth of Murray McLauchlan, singer-songwriter

JULY

Extra! Extra!

The Bulls Run in Spain

Each summer angry bulls chase hundreds of daredevils through the streets of Pamplona, Spain, to the city's bull ring. The death-defying race, called the "Running of the Bulls." is the highlight of the San Fermin festival. Runners slip and slide in this dangerous contest that takes the bulls only 2 1/2 minutes to complete. Once in the ring, the animals become part of the afternoon's bull fights.

The Tall Ships

During the summer of 1984, tourists travelled to Canadian ports to see the famous Tall Ships (schooners, brigs, clippers and barques) that represent the finest ships of the past. Some of the vessels have three masts, others are more than 90 m long. During the Quebec '84 celebrations, more than 50 Tall Ships docked at Vieux Port de Québec.

Trivia tidbit

Reading Rainbow, the children's T.V. show about books, attracted 6.5 million viewers each week in 1984.

What's *that*?!? Marshmallow

A marshmallow is a confection made of corn syrup, gelatin, sugar and starch. It was originally made from the root of the marsh mallow plant.

You said it!

"Don't bury your head in the sand." People believed that the ostrich buried its head in the sand, thinking that if it couldn't see the danger, it wasn't there. When we pretend not to see or hear the truth, we're hiding, too. (The ostrich is really swallowing sand for its digestion!)

Sunday 1 — *Canada Day*
From his home in Britain, Michael Adams, 12, beats Soviet chess star Gary Kasparov in the world's first exhibition match played by satellite.

Monday 2 — Karel Soucek of Hamilton, Ontario, goes over Niagara Falls in a homemade barrel that bounces on the rocks for nearly an hour before rescuers pull it safely to shore.
☆ 1821 — birth of Sir Charles Tupper, sixth prime minister of Canada

Tuesday 3 — At 119 years old, Shigechiyo Izumi of Tokunoshima, Japan, is the world's oldest person — two years older than Canada!
☆ 1870 — birth of Richard Bennett, 11th prime minister of Canada

JULY

Wednesday 4
In New York City, a ceremony is held as the Statue of Liberty's time-worn torch is lowered. It will be restored and returned in two years.

WORMS FOR SALE 75¢ 80¢

Thursday 5
Using crayons, Travis, 9, and Todd Harnden, 13, of Gore's Landing, Ontario, raise the prices on signs at their worm booth. Revenue officials informed them that they have to charge customers 7 per cent sales tax.
☆ **1943** — birth of Robbie Robertson, singer-songwriter

Friday 6
In Kansas City, Missouri, Michael Jackson and his family launch their 13-city, 37-performance Victory Tour for a sell-out crowd of 50 000.
☆ **1897** — birth of Charles Gorman, world champion speed skater

Saturday 7
John Candy, co-star of this summer's hit movie *Splash* has signed a three-movie deal with Walt Disney Pictures.
☆ **1969** — birth of Joe Sakic, hockey player

Sunday 8
Kelly-Ann Way of Windsor, Ontario, wins the 70-km eighth stage of the Tour de France women's cycling rally in 1 hour, 52 minutes and 39 seconds.
☆ **1948** — birth of Raffi (Cavoukian), singer-songwriter

Monday 9
Prime Minister John Turner calls a federal election for September 4.
☆ **1845** — birth of Gilbert J.M.K. Elliot, Earl of Minto, former governor general

Tuesday 10
Wayne Gretzky fans cheer as the Great One wins his third straight Seagram's Award as hockey player of the year.
☆ **1936** — birth of Lois Lilienstein, of Sharon, Lois & Bram

Wednesday 11
It's clean-up time! During showings of the hit film *Ghostbusters*, American audiences are pelting the screen with marshmallows when the villain, the Stay-puft Marshmallow man, appears.

Thursday 12
In the United States Democrat Geraldine Ferraro becomes the first woman in American history to be a major party vice-presidential candidate.

Friday 13
Food City has become the first Ontario grocery store chain to introduce children's shopping carts so kids can help with the family shopping.
☆ **1934** — birth of Peter Gzowski, radio host and writer

Saturday 14
In Toronto, Esto84, a cultural festival bringing together Estonians from around the world, ends after a week of sports, folkdancing and church services.

Sunday 15
Families are beating the summer heat in cool movie theatres showing *The Muppets Take Manhattan*, *The Last Starfighter*, and *The NeverEnding Story*.

Monday 16
Some Mongolians have discovered what scientists are calling a 3000-year-old Chinese computer. The calculating instrument is made of 20 thin ivory sticks (like chopsticks) that are used in an ancient mathematical system.

Tuesday 17
Pack your suitcase! Gerontologist Mary O'Brien says Prince Edward Islanders tend to live longer than people in other provinces.
☆ **1935** — birth of Donald Sutherland, actor

July

Wednesday 18
Some veggies are getting a lot of attention. Popular new items in stores and restaurants include radicchio, and gold, red, and purple peppers.

Thursday 19
Officials have discovered a $250 000 gold nugget in British Columbia. It had been hidden for 50 years in a provincial government vault.
☆ **1960** — birth of Atom Egoyan, film maker

Friday 20
No one takes first prize at the Canadian Hot Air Balloon Championships in Barrie, Ontario: none of the contestants was able to snatch a cup from the top of a flagpole while hovering above in a balloon.
☆ **1951** — birth of Paulette Bourgeois, author of the Franklin books

Saturday 21
Fifteen thousand fans welcome Bruce "the Boss" Springsteen as he kicks off his Canadian tour at the Montreal Forum.
☆ **1938** — birth of Anton Kuerti, pianist and composer

Sunday 22
A racehorse named Key to the Moon wins at the 125th running of the Queen's Plate at Woodbine Race Track in Toronto.
☆ **1940** — birth of Alex Trebek, host of *Jeopardy*

Monday 23
In London, experts are baffled by a long, skinny insect. So far they've been unable to identify it.

Tuesday 24
The remains of a 10 000-year-old campfire near Banff, Alberta, are being studied by a team of archaeologists who want to identify the early campers.

Wednesday 25
Soviet cosmonaut Svetlana Savitskaya becomes the first woman to walk in space as she works outside the orbiting *Salyut 7* space station for nearly four hours.
☆ **1957** — birth of Steve Podborski, world champion alpine skier

Thursday 26
Prince Philip visits Thompson, Manitoba, to present Duke of Edinburgh awards to young Canadians from the Prairie provinces who have excelled in public service.

Friday 27
Have a cuppa! A London department store is offering a special "New York Blend Tea" designed to suit the taste of New York City tap water.
☆ **1934** — birth of James Elder, champion equestrian

Saturday 28
Swimmer Alex Baumann carries the Canadian flag into the Los Angeles Coliseum during the opening ceremonies of the summer's Olympic Games.
☆ **1958** — birth of Terry Fox, Marathon of Hope runner

Sunday 29
In Toronto, Lin and Win Htut, Burmese boys joined at the abdomen, have been separated after 18 hours of surgery performed by a 43-member surgical team.

Monday 30
The musical version of Mordecai Richler's novel *The Apprenticeship of Duddy Kravitz* opens at the O'Keefe Centre in Toronto.
☆ **1942** — birth of Andrew Suknaski, poet

Tuesday 31
In Los Angeles, Canadian athletes have won three gold and three silver Olympic medals since the Games began three days ago.

AUGUST

Extra! Extra!

The Summer Olympics in Los Angeles

Hundreds of Canadian athletes marched into the Memorial Coliseum in Los Angeles for the closing ceremonies of the Games of the XXIII Olympiad. In a Hollywood-style spectacular, pop singer Lionel Richie sang a 12-minute version of his hit "All Night Long" and was joined by 200 breakdancers. While fireworks exploded overhead, the athletes formed human pyramids, and "See You in Seoul 1988" flashed on the scoreboard.

Top T.V. Programs 1984

- *Dynasty*
- *Dallas*
- *The Cosby Show*
- *60 Minutes*
- *Family Ties*
- *Simon & Simon*
- *The A-Team*
- *Knot's Landing*
- *Murder, She Wrote*
- *Crazy Like a Fox*
- *Falcon Crest*

Trivia tidbit

During the summer months, New Glasgow Lobster Suppers, a restaurant on Prince Edward Island, serves up to 1000 lobster dinners each day between 4:00 and 8:30 P.M.

You said it!

"There's a frog in my throat." Since the early 1900s, people have referred to a momentary hoarseness in their throat as a "frog," because the noise that results sounds like that animal's throaty croak.

What's *that*?!? Badlands

Badlands are dramatic, barren landscapes created when streams and rainstorms carve the soft rock into interesting shapes and leave little that supports life. Some of Canada's badlands, in southeastern Alberta, are famous for the dinosaur bones that have been exposed by erosion or by archaeologists.

AUGUST

Wednesday 1

Actor Paul Newman launches "Newman's Own Oldstyle Picture Show Popcorn," the latest in his line of edible products. All Newman food profits benefit charities around the world.
☆ **1905** — birth of Helen Hogg-Priestley, astronomer

Thursday 2

A delegation of Canadian athletes returns from the World Wheelchair Games in England with smashed world records and 35 gold medals.
☆ **1942** — birth of André Gagnon, pianist and composer

Friday 3

An international poll of critics and film makers has voted Claude Jutra's Québécois drama *Mon Oncle Antoine* the best movie ever produced in Canada.
☆ **1888** — birth of Margaret "Ma" Murray, newspaper publisher

Saturday 4

Digging continues in the Red Deer River badlands in Alberta. Scientists are excavating bonebed containing the remains of 50 horned dinosaurs called centrosauruses.
☆ **1877** — birth of Tom Thomson, painter

Sunday 5

On Prince Edward Island, the Charlottetown Festival celebrates the 1000th performance of the musical *Anne of Green Gables* with "Happy Birthday" and a candlelight dinner after the show.
☆ **1948** — birth of Sue Hammond, creator of *Beethoven Lives Upstairs*

Monday 6

It's the Civic Holiday in Manitoba, Saskatchewan, Northwest Territories and Ontario. And it's Heritage Day in Alberta. *And* Natal Day in Prince Edward Island and Nova Scotia. Elsewhere, it's New Brunswick Day and British Columbia Day!
☆ **1949** — birth of Mary di Michele, writer

Tuesday 7

Olympic medal up-date: Canada has collected another four gold, five silver, and seven bronze medals in swimming, diving, sculling, weightlifting and track at the Summer Games in Los Angeles.
☆ **1965** — birth of Elizabeth Manley, Olympic figure skater

Wednesday 8

Canadian canines drool at the thought of it: the Doggie Deli in Victoria. At Dan Kerr's store, owners can purchase doggie doughnuts, muffins and even birthday cakes made with a ground beef base. Future plans call for a special cheese drink.
☆ **1949** — birth of Patti Stren, author of *Hug Me*

Thursday 9

The popular movie *Revenge of the Nerds* has inspired the fashion-conscious. "Nerdy" kids are wearing heavy, dark-rimmed glasses, slicked-back hairdos, white socks and plastic pocket-protectors.
☆ **1964** — birth of Brett Hull, hockey player

Friday 10

John LaRocca has won the Bee Beard Contest held in Rhode Island. The beekeeper wore about 15 000 bees in a honey of a "beard" that covered his lower face, neck, chest and shoulders . . . and he wasn't stung even once!
☆ **1959** — birth of Florent Vollant of the singing duo Kashtin

AUGUST

Saturday
11
Some Vancouverites aren't worrying about mowing their lawns this summer — because they live year-round on floating homes, houses built on barges and docked on the city's shoreline.
☆ **1922** — birth of Mavis Gallant, writer

Sunday
12
The Summer Olympics close in Los Angeles. Canadian competitors brought home a total of 44 medals.
☆ **1904** — birth of Ken Watson, champion curler

Monday
13
Anne Ottenbrite, winner of gold, silver and bronze medals in the Olympic swimming pool, is honoured with a parade and the key to her hometown of Whitby, Ontario.
☆ **1938** — birth of Gene Plamondon, country singer and guitarist

Tuesday
14
Got-to-have toys in today's ads are the Michael Jackson microphone, the Mr. T action figure, Ballerina Sindy and Snake Mountain.
☆ **1962** — birth of Horst Bulau, ski jumper

Wednesday
15
Thousands of kids, anxious to ride roller coasters and munch cotton candy, hurry through the gates on opening day of the Canadian National Exhibition in Toronto.
☆ **1925** — birth of Oscar Peterson, jazz pianist

Thursday
16
Marilyn Bell unveils a plaque to open a park at the spot where she used to swim in Lake Ontario when she was 12 years old. In 1954, Bell became the first person to swim across the Great Lake.
☆ **1940** — birth of Linda Hutsell-Manning, author of *Animal Hours*

Friday
17
Back-to-school fashions for 1984 include striped jersey shirts, hooded pullovers and fleece clothing in teal, red and wine colours.
☆ **1961** — birth of Jamie Macoun, hockey player

Saturday
18
Gallons of uncooked batter dribble out from under the world's largest pancake — 6 m wide and 400 kg — when a helicopter and a crane flip the flapjack at an airport in Swanton, Vermont.
☆ **1893** — birth of Sir Ernest MacMillan, conductor and composer

Sunday
19
A full-colour portrait of U.S. president Ronald Reagan, made entirely of jelly beans (his favourite candy), is displayed at the Republican Convention Center in Dallas, Texas.
☆ **1969** — birth of Matthew Perry, actor

Monday
20
British Columbia's Debbie Brill wins the high-jump competition at a major international track and field meet in Nice, France.
☆ **1950** — birth of David Duke, composer

AUGUST

Tuesday 21
Clint Eastwood, the movies' number one box-office attraction, becomes the 169th celebrity to put his handprints in cement in front of Mann's Chinese Theatre in Hollywood.
☆ **1923** — birth of Robert William Stewart, research scientist

Wednesday 22
In Vancouver, Torontonian Gary Mugford is named Canada's Firefighter of the Year.
☆ **1943** — birth of Vlasta van Kampen, illustrator of *Rockanimals*

Thursday 23
Jason Calderon, 6, has caught a 13-kg chinook salmon in Lake Ontario. The boy reeled in the heavy fish himself off Port Credit.
☆ **1959** — birth of Nino Ricci, writer

Friday 24
Doctors at the Canadian Medical Association's annual meeting tell parents to stop worrying about teens' messy rooms. The experts say the mess is a sign of good health and of teens staking out their rights "like any other young animals."
☆ **1922** — birth of René Lévesque, politician and journalist

Saturday 25
Summer may be nearly over, but tourists are still flooding into the village of Peggy's Cove, Nova Scotia, a scenic spot painted and photographed more than any other place in Canada.

Sunday 26
Four nuns have been sent to Winnipeg by Mother Teresa to help organize the Missionaries of Charity's first Canadian mission.
☆ **1928** — birth of Peter Appleyard, jazz musician

Monday 27
Canadian actors Joe Flaherty and Dave Thomas are in Ontario filming a movie titled *Follow That Bird*. Co-stars include Big Bird and the rest of T.V.'s *Sesame Street* gang.

Tuesday 28
Members of the Royal Winnipeg Ballet are making final preparations for performances in Greece and Egypt.
☆ **1969** — birth of Jason Priestley, actor

Wednesday 29
Newspaper ads offer Michael Jackson fans items "inspired by you-know-who" on the singer's 26th birthday. The cost of the glitter socks and leather-look jacket and pants is $71.48 plus tax. A Jackson album or cassette is a bargain at $7.99.
☆ **1931** — birth of Lise Payette, broadcaster and writer

Thursday 30
Canadian astronaut (and hockey fan!) Marc Garneau, training in Texas for his October trip into space, shows the hockey puck he'll take with him. The puck will go on permanent display, somewhere on Earth, after the flight.
☆ **1896** — birth of Raymond Massey, actor

Friday 31
Marathoner Steve Fonyo brings his five-month-old Journey for Lives run for cancer research to Oshawa, Ontario.
☆ **1939** — birth of Dennis Lee, poet and author of *The Ice Cream Store*

Extra! Extra!

The Papal Visit to Canada

For the first time in the history of the Roman Catholic Church, a pope visited Canada.

During his visit, Pope John Paul II lit the Peace Flame in Toronto's Peace Garden and beatified Marie-Leonie Paradis, a 19th-century Quebec nun who founded the Little Sisters of the Holy Family.

The Mystery Remains

Sir John Franklin set out to explore the Arctic in 1845, but he and his crew never returned. Scientists are trying to solve the mystery of the Franklin expedition. The preserved, permafrosted bodies of some of Franklin's sailors found on Beechey Island were studied closely during the summer of 1984 and will hopefully provide some clues. After scientific samples were taken, the bodies were buried once more in the Arctic ice.

Trivia tidbit

The Great Wall of China, 2200 years old, is being repaired. The wall stretches more than 2400 km from Gansu to the Yellow Sea and is said to be the only man-made object visible from space.

What's *that*?!? Talking Stick

Some Native people believe that a "talking stick" gives the recipient the authority to speak on a public occasion.

You said it!

"I'll use my pin money." When straight pins were invented in the 13th century, they were scarce and expensive. Women saved any spare money (or an allowance from their husbands) until the one or two days during the year when pins were sold. Pins are cheaper today, but we still call money saved for a special, small expense "pin money."

Saturday 1 Stan Guignard of Callander, Ontario, has returned home from his trip around the world in a Model A Ford to raise money for cancer research.

Sunday 2 Canada Post releases two new stamps to mark the upcoming visit of Pope John Paul II to Canada.

Monday 3 At a news conference, astronaut Marc Garneau reveals he's been tumbled, twisted and whirled to prepare for his October trip into space aboard the *Challenger*.
☆ 1810 — birth of Paul Kane, artist

Tuesday 4 Canada gets a new prime minister as Brian Mulroney and the Conservative Party win the federal election with a landslide victory.

September

Wednesday 5
Actors Nicolas Cage and Christopher Plummer are in Gravenhurst, Ontario, making a movie about Edward "Ned" Hanlan, Canada's world champion rower.
☆ 1916 — birth of Frank Shuster, comedian and partner in Wayne and Shuster

Thursday 6
It's a father-son affair as actors Donald and Kiefer Sutherland attend the premiere of Kiefer's first film, *The Bay Boy*, at Toronto's Festival of Festivals.
☆ 1932 — birth of Gilles Tremblay, composer

Friday 7
Three Soviet cosmonauts aboard the *Salyut 7* space station set a space endurance record as they enter their 212th day in orbit around Earth.

Saturday 8
International Literacy Day
Nearly five thousand airmen from nine countries attend the Fourth Commonwealth Wartime Aircrew Reunion in Winnipeg.
☆ 1937 — birth of Barbara Frum, broadcast journalist

Sunday 9
Pope John Paul II arrives in Quebec City to begin a 12-day tour of Canada. Hundreds of children and Governor General Jeanne Sauvé greet the pontiff.

Monday 10
At the shrine of Ste.-Anne-de-Beaupré, Quebec, the Pope is met by 4000 Native people, some of whom have travelled for 20 hours for the occasion.
☆ 1907 — birth of Fay Wray, actor

Tuesday 11
Hear-yea! Hear-yea! Thirty-four costumed, international criers are entered in the annual Town Criers' Competition in Halifax.

Wednesday 12
The Pope visits the small town of Flat Rock, Newfoundland, and blesses the fleet.
☆ 1949 — birth of Kevin Major, author of *Eating Between the Lines*

Thursday 13
A Canadian woman has developed Baby Bell, a device that plays a song when a baby wets its diaper . . . and keeps playing until the baby has been changed!
☆ 1941 — birth of David Clayton-Thomas, singer-songwriter

Friday 14
Rabbi Tracy Guren Klirs of Winnipeg has become the first woman rabbi in Canada to have her own congregation.
☆ 1940 — birth of Barbara Greenwood, author of *A Pioneer Story*

Saturday 15
In London, Diana, Princess of Wales, gives birth to Henry Charles Albert David, a brother for two-year-old Prince William. The baby will be called Harry.
☆ 1901 — birth of Gweneth Lloyd, ballet choreographer

Sunday 16
The 102-storey Empire State Building is in darkness. Its 204 floodlights and 310 fluorescent lamps will be off until November while the skyscraper is rewired.

Monday 17
In Ottawa, Brian Mulroney is sworn in as the 18th prime minister of Canada. His 40-member cabinet includes six women ministers, the most ever.

Tuesday 18
Pope John Paul II visits Vancouver, where he receives a ceremonial talking stick from the elders of the Coast Salish Indian nation.
☆ 1895 — birth of John Diefenbaker, 13th prime minister of Canada

SEPTEMBER

Wednesday 19
Cheers abound as Team Canada wins the Canada Cup international hockey tournament in Edmonton with a nail-biting 6–5 win over Sweden.
☆ **1951** — birth of Daniel Lanois, composer and producer

Thursday 20
The Pope ends his tour of Canada with a day in Ottawa. He cruises down the Rideau Canal and is toasted by the Prime Minister at a farewell banquet.
☆ **1951** — birth of Guy Lafleur, hockey player

Friday 21
Amadeus, a movie about young Wolfgang Amadeus Mozart, is the hit of the film season. Mozart's music is playing everywhere, and the costumes influence fashion.
☆ **1934** — birth of Leonard Cohen, novelist and poet

Saturday 22
It's the first day of autumn, but kids who want to use their bicycles in Saskatoon have to pedal through early snow!

Sunday 23
Dishes rattle and residents of Moncton and Fredericton are jolted awake by an earthquake measuring about 4 on the Richter scale.
☆ **1946** — birth of Anne Wheeler, film maker

Monday 24
Queen Elizabeth II and Prince Philip land in Moncton to begin a two-week Canadian tour. They'll spend two days helping New Brunswickers celebrate their bicentennial in the Acadian town of Shediac.
☆ **1961** — birth of Nancy Garapick, world-record swimmer

Tuesday 25
The Children's Book Store in Toronto, the largest children's bookstore in the world, is celebrating its tenth anniversary with author readings, musical acts and plenty of Canadian children's books.
☆ **1933** — birth of Ian Tyson, singer-songwriter

Wednesday 26
Rosh Hashanah
Scientists claim that half the elementary school children in Japan don't know how to eat with chopsticks anymore. Stores are selling "trainer" chopsticks complete with loops that show children where to put their fingers.

Thursday 27
Queen Elizabeth tours eastern Ontario's Loyalist territory, settled in 1784. There she watches a re-enactment of the battle of Cornwall.
☆ **1937** — birth of Guido Basso, musician and composer

Friday 28
Carlton Cards has a new, noisy product — audio cards that use microchip technology. Tiny speakers deliver greetings to whoever opens the card. Designers are predicting cards will soon deliver the *sender's* voice.
☆ **1962** — birth of Grant Fuhr, hockey goalie

Saturday 29
The *Canadiana*, a derelict ferry that in its heyday shuttled millions of passengers between Buffalo, New York, and Ontario's Crystal Beach, has been towed to Buffalo to be restored as a maritime museum.
☆ **1946** — birth of Allen Morgan, author of *Ryan's Giant*

Sunday 30
The hot item in 1984 is the GoBot, a robot toy that changes into a car, truck, motorcycle, plane or spaceship when unfolded.

Extra! Extra!

Marc Garneau Blasts into History

On October 5, 1984, Marc Garneau became the first Canadian to enter space. Born in Quebec City in 1949, Garneau trained at Canadian military colleges, received a PhD in electrical engineering, and served as a naval officer. While in orbit, he studied the problems of nausea caused by zero gravity. His pre-flight training gave him plenty of experience — he was tumbled end over end and rotated in a chair!

Best-selling Albums in Canada 1984

♪ *Thriller*, Michael Jackson
♪ *Colour by Numbers*, Culture Club
♪ *Can't Slow Down*, Lionel Richie
♪ *Born in the USA,* Bruce Springsteen
♪ *Purple Rain,* Prince
♪ *She's So Unusual*, Cyndi Lauper
♪ *Sports*, Huey Lewis & the News
♪ *1984,* Van Halen
♪ *Footloose,* soundtrack
♪ *Eliminator*, ZZ Top

Trivia tidbit
The final tally's in. More than 13.6 million Canadians watched some part of the Pope's visit to Canada on television.

You said it!
"It's my swan song." People once believed, incorrectly, that a swan sings only once, beautifully, just before it dies. We call someone's last, wonderful performance or work (maybe before retirement, rather than death) a "swan song."

What's *that*?!? The Six Nations
Since the 1400s, five nations of Iroquois Native peoples have been linked by language and culture: the Senecas, Cayugas, Onondagas, Oneidas and Mohawks. In the 1750s a sixth nation, the Tuscaroras, joined them.

OCTOBER

Monday
1
Native children perform traditional dances for Queen Elizabeth II as she visits the Six Nations Reserve in Brantford, Ontario.
☆ **1926** — birth of Ben Wicks, cartoonist

Tuesday
2
The three Soviet cosmonauts who spent a record 237 days in space in an orbiting laboratory return safely to Earth.
☆ **1960** — birth of Glenn Anderson, hockey player

Wednesday
3
In Ottawa, Wayne Gretzky, Oscar Peterson, Robert Fulford and 71 other citizens receive the Order of Canada.
☆ **1882** — birth of Alexander Young (A.Y.) Jackson, Group of Seven painter

Thursday
4
Poet sean o'huigin has won the Canada Council Children's Literature Prize for *The Ghost Horse of the Mounties*. Laszlo Gal wins the illustration prize for *The Little Mermaid*, by Margaret Crawford Maloney.
☆ **1934** — birth of Rudy Wiebe, author

Friday
5
Yom Kippur
Marc Garneau becomes the first Canadian astronaut in space as the shuttle *Challenger* blasts off the launching pad at the Kennedy Space Center in Florida.

Saturday
6
In Winnipeg, Queen Elizabeth II watches 85 canoeists dressed as voyageurs re-enact the arrival of French explorer Pierre La Vérendrye 250 years ago.
☆ **1866** — birth of Reginald Fessenden, radio inventor

Sunday
7
Thanksgiving grocery shopping: turkey, $0.54 per kg; cranberries, $0.99 a bag; and pumpkin pie, $1.99 each.
☆ **1786** — birth of Louis-Joseph Papineau, orator and politician

Monday
8
Thanksgiving
A 256-kg Canadian beauty is runner-up in the World Pumpkin Federation's fourth annual World Weigh-off. Owen Woodman of Falmouth, Nova Scotia, is the proud owner of the gigantic gourd.
☆ **1929** — birth of Lois Smith, ballet dancer

Tuesday
9
"The view is absolutely extraordinary." Halfway through his mission, Marc Garneau speaks in French and English to the world from space.
☆ **1967** — birth of Carling Bassett-Seguso, tennis player

Wednesday
10
Torontonian Stephen Lewis has been named Canada's new ambassador to the United Nations.
☆ **1863** — birth of Louis Cyr, strongman

OCTOBER

Thursday
11

Front Page Challenge, Canadian T.V.'s longest running series, begins its 28th season with a live broadcast from Yellowknife, NWT.
☆ **1903** — birth of David Turner, world champion soccer player

Friday
12

Cross-country runner Steve Fonyo makes a stop in Hamilton, Ontario, to test an artificial leg designed especially for athletes. The prosthesis was inspired by Terry Fox during his Marathon of Hope.
☆ **1880** — birth of Healey Willan, composer-conductor

Saturday
13

The first-ever national 4-H calf competition for kids is held in Markham, Ontario. The calves will be judged on things such as the width of their rumps.
☆ **1955** — birth of Jane Siberry, singer-songwriter

Sunday
14

In Detroit, the Tigers beat the San Diego Padres 8–4 to win the World Series.
☆ **1927** — birth of Elmer Iseler, choir conductor

Monday
15

Twenty-two thousand light bulbs begin flashing on the world's largest electric sign as "Honest Ed" Mirvish opens his expanded Toronto department store.
☆ **1908** — birth of John Kenneth Galbraith, economist

Tuesday
16

In London, Anne Murray is taping her new T.V. special, "Sounds of London." Guests include her singer brother Bruce, Dusty Springfield and Miss Piggy.
☆ **1870** — birth of Wallace Turnbull, aeronautical engineer

Wednesday
17

Wild whooping cranes are mating in record numbers at nesting sites in Wood Buffalo National Park on the Alberta-Northwest Territories border. If all goes well, there will be more than 100 of the endangered birds by the end of 1985.
☆ **1948** — birth of Margot Kidder, actor

Thursday
18

Canadian chefs become the world champions of cooking at the World Culinary Olympics in Frankfurt, Germany. It's the first time since the competition began in 1896 that chefs from one country have won in all categories and disciplines!
☆ **1919** — birth of Pierre Elliott Trudeau, 15th prime minister of Canada

Friday
19

Ducks, the season's most popular motif, are appearing on many household items, including linens, wallpaper, dishes and clothing.
☆ **1939** — birth of Tommy Ambrose, singer-songwriter

Saturday
20

Anglican bishop Desmond Tutu, a crusader against apartheid in South Africa, has won the Nobel Peace Prize.
☆ **1873** — birth of Nellie McClung, suffragist and legislator

Sunday
21

The Canadian Academy of Recording Arts and Sciences nominates Bryan Adams for seven Juno Awards; Corey Hart, Fred Penner and the Rugrats are fellow nominees.
☆ **1863** — birth of John Clarence Webster, physician and historian

OCTOBER

Monday 22
Dennis Lee and his friend Phil Balsam are busy writing the words and tunes for Gobo, Wembley, Mokey and Boober, characters on the kids' T.V. show *Fraggle Rock*.
☆ **1844** — birth of Louis Riel, Métis leader and founder of Manitoba

Tuesday 23
Mountain gear hits the city streets. Style-conscious folks are wearing heavy, thick-soled hiking boots, tied with long laces.
☆ **1885** — birth of Lawren Harris, Group of Seven painter

Wednesday 24
India opens Calcutta's first subway. The air-conditioned four-car train is part of a system designed to carry up to 7000 passengers every hour.
☆ **1929** — birth of Normie Kwong, football player

Thursday 25
Teed off? No! George Knudson and Al Balding have been elected to the Canadian Golf Hall of Fame.
☆ **1949** — birth of Laurie Grant Skreslet, first Canadian to climb Mount Everest

Friday 26
The Canadian Toy Testing Council has released its annual Toy Report. Tops on the list for safety and kid appeal are Gloworm and Globug, and Cabbage Patch Kids and Preemies.
☆ **1951** — birth of Willie P. Bennett, singer-songwriter

Saturday 27
A San Francisco jeweller has created a gold-plated gumball machine gleaming with 8 diamonds, 65 sapphires, 65 rubies, and other gems. What's inside? Plain ol' gumballs.
☆ **1928** — birth of Gilles Vigneault, singer-songwriter

Sunday 28
Teen Sukhbir Dhillon of Toronto sets a world record as he scampers up the 1760 steps of the CN Tower in 9 minutes, 45 seconds during the United Way's seventh annual Hallowe'en Rock Walk.
☆ **1938** — birth of Gary Cowan, champion amateur golfer

Monday 29
Jennifer Nielsen, 8, of Vancouver, is the first Canadian to receive one of 12 Foreign Minister awards in the annual International Children's Art Exhibition in Japan. Nearly 15 000 entries were received from 77 countries.
☆ **1926** — birth of Jon Vickers, opera singer

Tuesday 30
Olympic gold-medal swimmer Alex Baumann has agreed to a two-year contract to promote eggs for the Canadian Egg Marketing Agency. He'll appear in T.V. and radio commercials, and on billboards.
☆ **1953** — birth of Robin Muller, author-illustrator of *Little Wonder*

Wednesday 31
Hallowe'en
In New Delhi, Indian prime minister Indira Gandhi is assassinated. Her son Rajiv is sworn in as the new prime minister and appeals for calm in the country.
☆ **1950** — birth of John Candy, actor

Extra! Extra!

Cyclist Halfway on Round World Trip

Richard Beecroft of Ontario, who suffers from multiple sclerosis, is raising awareness of the disease by cycling around the world. He left Toronto on his 10-speed tricycle in September 1983 and has now reached Athens, his halfway point around the globe. Yoga, a vegetarian diet and the generosity of people he meets help Beecroft as he heads for home. Expected arrival in Toronto: September 1986.

A Pilgrimage to India

In November 1984, India's Roman Catholic community celebrated the biggest event in the church calendar: the once-in-a-decade display of the body of St. Francis Xavier, who died 442 years earlier. In 55 days, nearly half a million people from all over the world filed past the glass coffin inside the Se Cathedral in Old Goa.

Trivia tidbit

At the Los Angeles Olympics, the more than 7000 athletes ate 125 476 kg of bananas and 20 828 kg of T-bone steaks in only 15 days.

What's *that*?!? Throne Speech

Traditionally, the Throne Speech (or, Speech from the Throne) is read by the governor general. It outlines the direction a new session of Parliament will take.

You said it!

"Get your feet wet first."
A swimmer may test the water temperature by dipping a toe into the pool before jumping in. When you're in a new situation, you get "your feet wet" by taking things slowly and getting a feel for the job. You're "testing the water," too.

NOVEMBER

Thursday
1
Leonard Cohen's music video special *I Am a Hotel* has won two more prizes: at the New York International Film & T.V. Festival and the Yorkton, Saskatchewan, festival.
☆ **1932** — birth of Al Cherney, fiddler

Friday
2
Banff, Jasper, Yoho and Kootenay national parks in the Rockies have been designated as a World Heritage Site by the United Nations Educational, Scientific and Cultural Organization.
☆ **1961** — birth of k.d. lang, singer-songwriter

Saturday
3
Five-time world professional wrestling champion "Whipper" Billy Watson receives an honorary doctor of laws degree from York University in Ontario in recognition of his work for many charities.
☆ **1925** — birth of Monica Hughes, author of *The Golden Aquarians*

Sunday
4
A giant red mailbox, symbolizing Canada Post's Santa Letter Reply program, leads Toronto's annual Santa Claus Parade of 20 floats and 21 marching bands.
☆ **1881** — birth of Gena Branscombe, composer-conductor

Monday
5
In Ottawa, Governor General Jeanne Sauvé reads the Throne Speech in the Senate chamber and opens the 33rd Parliament.
☆ **1959** — birth of Bryan Adams, singer-songwriter

Tuesday
6
Ronald Reagan is elected to a second term as president of the United States after a landslide win in 49 of the 50 states.

Wednesday
7
Temperatures in Red Deer, Alberta, have plunged to −26°C, forcing officials to use hatchets to free grebes trapped in frozen ponds. The birds thaw out in nearby warm garages.
☆ **1955** — birth of Shirley Eikhard, singer-songwriter

Thursday
8
Statistics Canada reports that households in Saskatchewan spend twice as much on toilet bowl cleaners as people in British Columbia. Authorities can't explain why.
☆ **1940** — birth of Janet Foster, author and naturalist

Friday
9
Tracey-Lynn Provost, 11, of Hemmingford, Quebec, receives a Medal of Bravery at Government House in Ottawa. The young hero rescued her 3-year-old brother from a fire last year.
☆ **1717** — birth of Louis-Joseph Gaultier de La Vérendrye, explorer

Saturday
10
Manitoba announces it will raise its minimum wage by 30 cents in 1985. The new hourly rate of $4.30 will be the highest in the country.
☆ **1845** — birth of Sir John Thompson, fourth prime minister of Canada

NOVEMBER

Sunday
11

Remembrance Day
In Oita, Japan, André Viger of Sherbrooke, Quebec, and Mel Fitzgerald of St. John's, Newfoundland, finish first and second in the 42-km International Wheelchair Marathon.
☆ **1935** — birth of Kathleen Shannon, film maker

Monday
12

It's c-c-c-o-l-d in Yellowknife, NWT. Temperatures of –34°C mean the ferry across the Mackenzie River has had to be lifted out of the water earlier than usual. In a few weeks, the ice will be thick enough to drive over.
☆ **1925** — birth of Agnes Nanogak, graphic artist

Tuesday
13

In Washington, DC, former prime minister Pierre Trudeau receives the Albert Einstein Peace Prize for his efforts to ease tensions between the superpowers last year.
☆ **1940** — birth of Bonnie Dobson, singer-songwriter

Wednesday
14

The last full-sized car to be built at the General Motors plant in Oshawa, Ontario, has come off the assembly line: Chevrolet Caprice Classic, no. 4 031 806. The plant will be closed down and rebuilt to produce smaller cars.
☆ **1949** — birth of Carol Matas, author of *Sworn Enemies*

Thursday
15

Olympic gold-medal diver Sylvie Bernier films the CTV show "Thrill of a Lifetime" at the Etobicoke Olympium in Ontario. In the show, Bernier helps a young swimmer learn to jump off the 10-m board.
☆ **1969** — birth of Helen Kelesi, champion tennis player

Friday
16

Tim Earley, 15, and his Angus steer win the grand prize in the Queen's Guineas competition at the Royal Agricultural Winter Fair in Toronto. Tim's dad won the same contest 25 years ago!
☆ **1957** — birth of Barbara Reid, author-illustrator of *Two by Two*

Saturday
17

Kids' writers Robert Munsch, Eric Wilson and Dennis Lee read at Toronto's Roy Thomson Hall to launch the eighth annual Children's Book Festival. More authors will be touring Canada all week.
☆ **1939** — birth of Gordon Lightfoot, singer-songwriter

Sunday
18

In Edmonton, the Winnipeg Blue Bombers defeat the Hamilton Tiger-Cats, 47–17, to win the 72nd Grey Cup.
☆ **1927** — birth of Knowlton Nash, journalist

Monday
19

The Canadian government has donated $50 million to drought-ravaged Africa, where 35 million people are starving. Shipments of food, medicine and relief vehicles are on the way.
☆ **1846** — birth of Octavius Newcombe, piano maker

Tuesday
20

On June 8, 1984, one hundred of Canada's finest photographers took pictures across the country. The resulting book, *A Day in the Life of Canada*, is on bookstore shelves today.
☆ **1841** — birth of Sir Wilfrid Laurier, seventh prime minister of Canada

NOVEMBER

Wednesday
21

Detroit hockey fans cheer as Gordie Howe's retired number 9 is hoisted to the rafters of Joe Louis Arena and Howe is admitted to the Detroit Red Wings' Hall of Fame.
☆ **1902** — birth of Foster Hewitt, hockey broadcaster

Thursday
22

VidKids, a lively show featuring singer Bob Schneider, wins best variety program under 30 minutes at the annual Canadian Film & Television Association Awards.
☆ **1950** — birth of Linda Granfield, the author of this book

Friday
23

During a visit to Hiroshima, Japan, Mother Teresa prays and places a wreath at the cenotaph for victims of the atomic bomb dropped at the end of World War II.
☆ **1817** — birth of William Brydone Jack, astronomer

Saturday
24

Two thousand kids ride the Santa Claus Express from northern Ontario towns to "the North Pole," where Santa boards the train, gives goodies and collects wish lists. The passengers are chaperoned on the free trip by nurses and firefighters because NO parents are allowed!
☆ **1940** — birth of Eric Wilson, author of *The St. Andrews Werewolf*

Sunday
25

In West Berlin, Gaëtan Boucher of Quebec wins the men's overall speed skating title at the world sprint competition. He won by eight one-hundredths of a second!
☆ **1888** — birth of Alfred Charpentier, labour leader

Monday
26

In Montreal, National Hockey League superstar Guy Lafleur announces his retirement. "The Flower" played for five Stanley Cup championship teams in the 1970s and leaves with 1246 career points.
☆ **1933** — birth of Robert Goulet, singer-actor

Tuesday
27

U.S. Olympic weightlifter Kevin Winter trains hard — and munches more than 1000 candy bars and 6 kg of powdered chocolate in milkshakes every year. (No zits, either!)
☆ **1943** — birth of Nicole Brossard, poet

Wednesday
28

Former Beatle Paul McCartney receives the "Freedom of Liverpool" (a plaque and a small key) during a visit to the English city that was home to the popular singing group in the 1960s.
☆ **1851** — birth of Albert Henry Grey, former governor general and donor of football's Grey Cup

Thursday
29

Christmas is coming . . . and Pound Puppies, the squishable stuffed cloth dogs, are inviting themselves into kids' homes via catalogue pages and television commercials.
☆ **1949** — birth of Stan Rogers, singer-songwriter

Friday
30

Steve Fonyo lays a garland of British Columbia holly at the foot of the Terry Fox statue in Thunder Bay, Ontario. Like Fox before him, Fonyo is running to raise funds for cancer research.
☆ **1872** — birth of John McCrae, author of "In Flanders Fields"

DECEMBER

Extra! Extra!

How Much Are the Twelve Days of Christmas?

In 1984, if you're in the market for twelve drummers drumming, eleven pipers piping, ten lords a-leaping, nine dancers dancing, eight maids a-milking, seven swans a-swimming, six geese a-laying, five gold rings, four calling birds, three French hens, two turtle doves and a partridge in a pear tree, you'll need $48 912.40 — and a *very* large shopping cart!

Top Toys

The most popular toys of the 1984 holiday season include Cabbage Patch dolls, Transformers that change from trucks into robots, Masters of the Universe action figures and My Little Pony.

Trivia tidbit

Astronaut Marc Garneau estimated he'd signed almost 10 000 autographs during two weeks of touring Canada's provincial capitals in 1984.

What's *that*?!? *Challah*

Challah is a traditional Jewish bread made with eggs and leavened with yeast. The braided loaf is eaten on the Sabbath and on holidays.

You said it!

"It's straight from the horse's mouth." Throughout history, buyers have examined a horse's teeth to determine its age and health, rather than relying on the word of the trader. When you have something "from the horse's mouth," you've got it from the source, or on good authority.

DECEMBER

Saturday
1
Just in time for Christmas . . . a kid-sized, gas-powered Mercedes-Benz for $1100. (Gas not included.)
☆ **1880** — birth of Thomas Taylor, explorer

Sunday
2
Governor General Jeanne Sauvé is made a companion of the Order of the Red Cross in recognition of her distinguished service to the people of Canada.
☆ **1885** — birth of J.-J. Gagnier, composer-conductor

Monday
3
In Dallas, Winnipeger Bruce McKay wins the White Rock Marathon, running the 26 miles in 2 hours, 20 minutes and 20 seconds.
☆ **1936** — birth of John Arpin, pianist

Tuesday
4
In New York, a teenage couple, grandchildren of a prestigious rabbi, are married during what is billed as the biggest wedding in history. The 30 000 invited guests are served 7 tonnes of cake and a 100-kg challah 5 m long.
☆ **1921** — birth of Deanna Durbin, actor

Wednesday
5
Bryan Adams wins four Juno Awards with his *Cuts Like a Knife* album. The Rugrats win Best Children's Album for *Rugrat Rock*.
☆ **1875** — birth of Sir Arthur Currie, World War I commander

Thursday
6
Saskatchewan is planning to send about 20 000 tonnes of wheat to drought-stricken African nations.
☆ **1961** — birth of Stephane Poulin, author-illustrator of *Endangered Animals*

Friday
7
Swiss + watch = Swatch, the latest in fashionable accessories. Some models are scented strawberry or lollipop, and colours range from fluorescent to totally transparent.
☆ **1916** — birth of Jean "Ti-Jean" Carignan, fiddler

Saturday
8
Need a lift? Stan Reynold of Wetaskiwin, Alberta, has more than 4000 antique vehicles — plows, sleighs, cars, fire engines, tractors and steam engines — on exhibit in a museum he has built.
☆ **1909** — birth of Gratien Gélinas, actor

Sunday
9
Earth tremors shake houses near Bathurst, New Brunswick, as a small quake hits 3.5 on the Richter scale.
☆ **1935** — birth of Christopher Pratt, artist

Monday
10
Bob Homme, T.V.'s Friendly Giant, tapes his last episode. He's played the character for 31 years and to three generations of T.V. viewers in the U.S. and Canada.
☆ **1928** — birth of John Colicos, actor

Tuesday
11
The 2500 people in the Baffin Island community of Frobisher Bay have voted to change the name of the town back to Iqaluit, which means "fish" in the Inuktitut language.
☆ **1948** — birth of Tony Gabriel, football player

DECEMBER

Wednesday
12
Fake Cabbage Patch dolls are being seized, tested and banned in the United States and Canada. Officials say the counterfeit dolls are flammable; the real dolls are safe.

Thursday
13
Canada Post reports that children have already made 370 000 phone calls to Santa Claus on the North Pole hotline. Kids can talk to Santa in either French or English. *Joyeux Noël!*
☆ **1929** — birth of Christopher Plummer, actor

Friday
14
Woof! Six thousand dogs from around the world are in Toronto for the Credit Valley Kennel & Obedience Club Dog Show, Canada's largest indoor dog show.
☆ **1954** — birth of Stephen MacLean, astronaut

Saturday
15
Two 7000-year-old human brains have been found in skulls unearthed near the space shuttle launch site in Florida.
☆ **1878** — birth of Robert Medrum, astronomer

Sunday
16
The Canadian Forces have delivered eight Christmas trees to a group of Inuit children living near the North Pole, hundreds of kilometres above the treeline. For many, these are the first trees they've ever seen.
☆ **1938** — birth of John Allan Cameron, singer

Monday
17
Olympic gold-medal diver Sylvie Bernier of Montreal announces her retirement as a competitive swimmer. She will advise the federal Department of Fitness and Amateur Sport.
☆ **1874** — birth of William Lyon Mackenzie King, 10th prime minister of Canada

Tuesday
18
Alex Baumann is named the Canadian Press male athlete of 1984, edging out Gaëtan Boucher and ending Wayne Gretzky's four-year hold on the award.
☆ **1961** — birth of Brian Orser, Olympic figure skater

Wednesday
19
Chanukah
Wayne Gretzky collects his 1000th career point two minutes into the Edmonton Oilers' game against the Los Angeles Kings. He's the 18th player in NHL history to achieve the mark, but he did it at a younger age and quicker pace than those before him.
☆ **1924** — birth of Doug Harvey, hockey player

Thursday
20
South African Bishop Desmond Tutu, winner of the 1984 Nobel Peace Prize, arrives in Toronto for a brief visit with religious leaders and activist groups working for racial equality in his homeland.
☆ **1924** — birth of Julia "Judy" LaMarsh, politician and writer

Friday
21
In Ottawa, the Order of Canada list is announced: honours will be presented to Marc Garneau and Olympians Alex Baumann, Victor Davis, Anne Ottenbrite and Laurence Cain.
☆ **1930** — birth of Claire Mackay, author of *Touching All the Bases*

December

Saturday
22

British prime minister Margaret Thatcher, after consultation with the Queen and literary societies, names Ted Hughes (author of *The Iron Man*) Britain's new poet laureate.
★ **1969** — birth of Myriam Bedard, Olympic biathlete

Sunday
23

A chef at a Boston hotel finishes trimming a gigantic gingerbread house that will be a gift to the neighbourhood children. The house is built of 150 kg of gingerbread, 125 kg of icing and $1400 worth of candies.
★ **1929** — birth of Patrick Watson, T.V. personality

Monday
24

The first Godzilla film appeared in 1954 — and 30 years later, the Japanese monster is still inspiring movies. The latest flick features a computerized Godzilla that can roll its eyes, bare its fangs, and belch flames.
★ **1903** — birth of Jack Purcell, world champion badminton player

Tuesday
25

Christmas

Queen Elizabeth II's annual holiday greeting includes film footage of her grandson Prince Harry's christening. Meanwhile in Rome, Pope John Paul II wishes the world a Happy Christmas in 47 languages.
★ **1900** — birth of Edgar Steacie, research chemist

Wednesday
26

Boxing Day

Thirty-three previously unknown works by Johann Sebastian Bach have been discovered at Yale University. They are believed to have been written before 1710 — and have music experts around the world *very* excited.
★ **1937** — birth of Ronnie Prophet, singer

Thursday
27

The world's first artificial comet makes its debut 100 000 km out in space. Clouds prevent most viewers from seeing the colourful flash and its 40 000-km tail.
★ **1823** — birth of Sir Mackenzie Bowell, fifth prime minister of Canada

Friday
28

As they have since the 1960s, workers are clearing and packing snow to make more than 1000 km of Canada's coldest and toughest highways, across Great Bear and Contwoyto Lakes, north of Yellowknife, NWT. Each April, the ice roads melt.
★ **1763** — birth of John Molson, brewer

Saturday
29

Soviet archaeologists have unearthed a 105-million-year-old nest of unbroken dinosaur eggs on the slopes of the Fergana mountain range in Central Asia.
★ **1963** — birth of Lisa Savijarvi, world champion alpine skier

Sunday
30

Astronomers are jumping with joy after spotting for the first time what is believed to be a planet outside the solar system orbiting a faint star about 21 light-years from Earth.
★ **1943** — birth of Linda Thom, Olympic target shooter

Monday
31

Celebrations marking the 200th anniversary of Cape Breton Island's founding as a British colony begin at the stroke of midnight. Happy Birthday — and Happy New Year!
★ **1947** — birth of Burton Cummings, singer-songwriter